ASIA MINOR

KAPPADOCIA

CYPRUS

MEDITERRANEAN
SEA

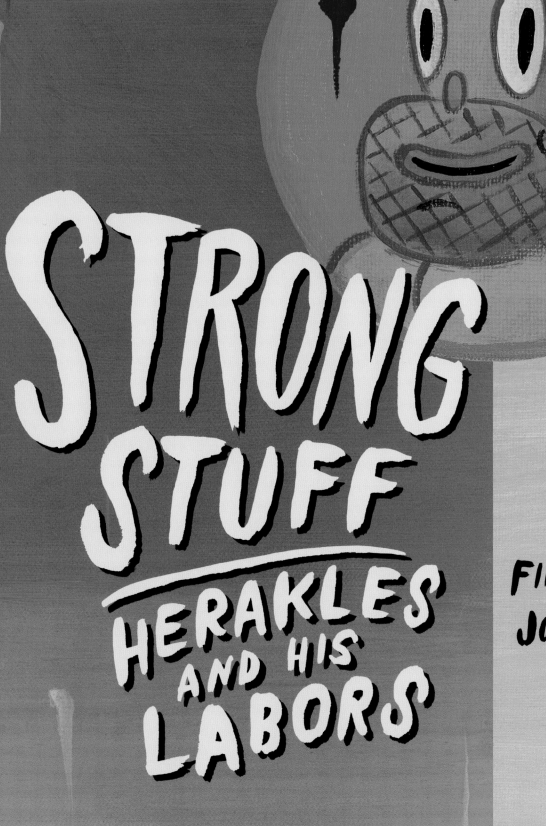

STRONG STUFF

HERAKLES AND HIS LABORS

FIERCE WORDS BY JOHN HARRIS

POWERFUL ART BY GARY BASEMAN

THE J. PAUL GETTY MUSEUM   LOS ANGELES

Table of Labors

I

THE NEMEAN LION

II

THE HIND OF KERYNEIA

III

THE ERYMANTHIAN BOAR

IV

THE LERNAEAN HYDRA

V

THE STYMPHALIAN BIRDS

VI

THE AUGEAN STABLES

VII

THE CRETAN BULL

VIII

THE HORSES OF DIOMEDES

IX

THE GIRDLE OF THE AMAZONS

X

THE OXEN OF GERYON

XI

CERBERUS

XII

THE GOLDEN APPLES
OF THE HESPERIDES

OUR STORY BEGINS

THE TIME: Long, long ago.

THE PLACE: Greece and far beyond: up to Mount Olympos, home of the gods and goddesses; down to Hades, the spooky land of the dead.

BACKGROUND INFO: Herakles, the most famous of all heroes, performed a number of famous labors—tasks, jobs, what have you. Why? Because of Hera, the Queen of Olympos, who never, ever gave Herakles a break. She hated Herakles because he was one of the many children her husband, Zeus, had had with other women. She even tried to kill Herakles as a baby, by sending snakes into his crib, which he strangled with his bare baby hands. This only made Hera MORE angry, and when the baby grew up, she played a horrible trick on him. But the results of her cruel trick backfired in a funny way. Thanks to Hera, Herakles made the world a more livable place by removing terrifying creatures and major nuisances, sometimes using his brawn (which was considerable), sometimes using his brain. No wonder the Greeks loved him so!

Herakles was married to a nice lady, and they had children. One day Hera decided to send the Fury of Madness down from Mount Olympos. Destination: Herakles.

The Fury of Madness did what you would expect her to do: she drove Herakles into a state of craziness, one that was so extreme that he killed his poor wife and children.

Horrified at what he had done and looking for help, Herakles decided to consult the famous Oracle at Delphi, an old crone who would sniff magic fumes and utter strange statements that sometimes made sense (but more often did not).

The Oracle told Herakles he would have to go to King Eurystheus of Mycenae and do anything the king asked for a period of twelve long years.

The king decided to give Herakles a series of tasks that came to be called his "labors." These were super-difficult jobs that the king hoped would defeat the great hero. Or kill him! (Herakles was the king's cousin and rival for the throne.) But as we'll soon see, the king was going to be unpleasantly surprised by our hero's survival skills.

HOW'S THAT AGAIN?

Delphi **DEL-fee**
Eurystheus **yoo-RISS-thee-yoos**
Hades **HAY-dees**
Hera **HEER-ah**
Herakles **HARE-ah-kleez***
Mycenae **my-SEE-nee**
Olympos **oh-LIM-pos**
Zeus **Zoose**

* The Romans called him "Hercules," but we're using his original Greek name here.

I. THE NEMEAN LION

ASSIGNMENT: *Kill it.*

First up, the Nemean Lion—which of course looks like the "Mean Lion."

How mean was the Nemean Lion? Well, he had been on a rampage in the countryside around Nemea. (Find it on the map in the front of this book. It's there!)

He was one tough lion: his skin was so thick, no arrow could pierce it. Ditto spears. Ditto Herakles' trusty sword.

What to do? Herakles was really stumped.

Then one day he had a brainstorm and realized that—since he couldn't use a bow and arrow or anything else—he'd just have to tough it out with the roaring beast, *mano a mano,** or "mano a paw," so to speak.

He tracked the Nemean Lion down to its cave, went inside, and strangled it with his big bare hands. The animal protested, needless to say; but, before too long, out walked Herakles, holding the skin of the Nemean Lion—a kind of gross souvenir that he had cut off the no-longer-living beast by using its own claw as a razor.

In his later adventures, Herakles wore this lion's skin, partly for good luck, partly because it was so tough (no arrows, no spears, remember?), and partly because—let's face it—it looked so good on his extremely athletic body.

You often see Herakles wearing the skin of the Nemean Lion in works of art; it's tied around his neck in a knot known as—guess what?— a Herakles knot. He probably even wore it when he was just lounging around in Athens, or Thebes, or Olympos, or wherever.

*Meaning: *Hand to hand.*

HOW'S THAT AGAIN?

Nemea **neh-MAY-ah**
Nemean **neh-MAY-an**
Thebes **THEEBS**

II. THE HIND OF KERYNEIA

ASSIGNMENT: *Bring back her horn.*

Our hero spent a whole year on this labor.

First, Herakles had to find out what a hind was: "the female of the red deer." So far, so good.

Then he had to find out where Keryneia was. That took a while. (If only he'd had our handy map!)

Finally Herakles cornered the hind in question. She was fairly easy to spot, given that she had two golden horns and four hooves of bronze.

Before you could say "Keryneia," that hind was missing a horn. Ouch!

And so King Eurystheus found himself in possession of a golden horn that he didn't really want in the first place.

HOW'S THAT AGAIN?

Keryneia
kay-ree-NAY-ah

III. THE ERYMANTHIAN BOAR

ASSIGNMENT: *Bring him back.*

The Erymanthian Boar, who lived in Erymanthos, was a very big pig with absolutely no manners; in fact, he was on a rampage, and Herakles had to find him and bring him back alive.

Herakles chased and chased and chased the big wild pig until finally it just had to sit down. Herakles seized his chance and sat down, too. Then, rested, they continued on, until, completely pooped, the boar had some kind of seizure and Herakles picked him up in his big arms.

By the time the boar woke up, it was too late: he was in Mycenae, where—to his embarrassment—he had been scratched off the list of labors.

When Herakles returned—again!—Eurystheus freaked out and hid in a big jar. Just for fun, our hero picked up the boar and held it over the mouth of the jar, pretending he was going to drop it inside.

Ha-ha-ha, Eurystheus!

HOW'S THAT AGAIN?

Erymanthian
Air-ee-MAN-thee-an

Erymanthos
Air-ee-MAN-thos

Mycenae
my-SEE-nee

IV. THE LERNAEAN HYDRA

ASSIGNMENT: *Get rid of it.*

The Lernaean Hydra, for starters, had so many vowels in its name that it hardly knew what to do. Well, that's not really true: its goal in life was to terrify the countryside around Lerna. (Check the map, again.)

What was so terrifying about this hydra? Well, it had many, many heads, and each one exhaled really bad breath—so bad that to breathe it was fatal for anyone in the vicinity. Gross. (A word to the wise: *Avoid hydra breath.*)

AND if you cut off one of the hydra's heads, it grew back TWO—two heads with fatal breath. Horrible, but—let's face it—impressive.

Herakles finally came up with a plan that was pretty neat but pretty gruesome. First, he chopped off each head (an obvious first step). Next, he took a red-hot "brand"—think of it as a torch—and seared the STUMP where the head had been. Whoa!

THEN he dipped his arrows in the horrible blood pouring out everywhere—and believe me, you wouldn't want to be on the receiving end of one of THOSE arrows.

Chop, chop, chop…sear, sear, sear…dip, dip, dip.

Finally, Herakles was down to one head—the immortal head of the hydra. It's really tough, if not impossible, to kill an immortal head. So he buried it under a big rock: the bigger the better, if you ask me.

HOW'S
THAT
AGAIN?

Hydra **HI-dra**
Lernaean **ler-NAI-an**

V. THE STYMPHALIAN BIRDS

ASSIGNMENT: *Get rid of them.*

Nasty: these birds had beaks and wings of iron. You would never, ever want to mess with a Stymphalian Bird—not if you knew what was good for you.

The birds lived around Lake Stymphalos. They were a menace, and no one knew what to do.

Enter Herakles.

Now, these scary metal birds flocked together; think of the noise when they bumped up against each other! Clang, clang…

Well, this gave Herakles a bright idea. He got hold of some big metal cymbals and BANGED them together. KERRR—ASHHHHH!!!! And the sound was so awful it scared the Stymphalian Birds—even Stymphalian Birds can get scared, you know, frightening as they themselves are—and off they flew in all directions, scattering.

This meant that Herakles could now go after them one by one—a much easier proposition. He got out his bow and arrow, and—ker-boing!—one less Stymphalian Bird! He kept at it until the few birds left alive decided to split from Lake Stymphalos. Goodbye, Stymphalian Birds! Wherever you are, I hope you stay there!

HOW'S THAT AGAIN?

Stymphalos STIM-fah-los
Stymphalian stim-FAY-lee-an

VI. THE AUGEAN STABLES

ASSIGNMENT: *Clean them out. Ick.*

Pretty gross.

OK. Augeas was the king of Elis (find it on the map!), and he had these huge, huge stables where he kept lots and lots and lots of cows. LOTS of cows.

Augeas was lazy, or cheap, or both, and didn't bother to CLEAN OUT the stables. It didn't take very long before the stables were…well, you can imagine.

Now, Herakles' little task was to clean out the filthy stables of Augeas—a revolting task—and—get this—he had to finish this smelly labor in ONE DAY.

What to do?

Herakles sat down and thought and thought and thought and thought. What was he thinking?

Well, our hero knew that he would need water—a LOT of water—to flush out those stables. But where would he get it?

Answer: a river! The River Alpheus, to be precise, which—fortunately—was nearby and simply *brimming* with water.

So, Herakles pushed and pulled and dug and—frankly, I don't know what he did, exactly, but everyone agrees that he "diverted" the river, not in the sense of showing the River Alpheus a good time but in the sense of making it change direction.

So the river, redirected, flowed right through the stables of King Augeas, and, before you knew it, all that muck and guck was flushed right out.

Labor accomplished, and in one day, too.

HOW'S THAT AGAIN?

Alpheus **AI-FEE-us**
Augean **aw-GEE-an**
Augeas **aw-GEE-as**
Elis **EE-lis**

VII. THE CRETAN BULL

ASSIGNMENT: *Bring him back.*

This was, of course, a bull, and he did indeed live on
the island of Crete, where he ran around, making
life miserable for anyone unlucky enough to get in his way. Or
even near his way. According to one ancient authority, he "created
havoc." Havoc is no laughing matter, especially when you're on an
island, like Crete, and it's hard to get off and it's easy for
the Cretan Bull to find you.

Some say Herakles captured the bull alive; to make
matters worse (for the bull), Herakles even rode him
all the way back to Mycenae, home base for King
Eurystheus. The king was not too happy to see
Herakles riding up on the Cretan Bull!

Once on the mainland of Greece, the bull
took up residence near Marathon, where he
lived contentedly for many years—until
the great hero Theseus killed him.

HOW'S
THAT AGAIN?
Cretan **KREET-an**
Crete **KREET**
Mycenae **my-SEE-nee**
Theseus **THEE-see-us**

VIII. THE HORSES OF DIOMEDES

ASSIGNMENT: *Bring them back.*

These extremely awful horses belonged to King Diomedes of Thrace. He was the son of Ares, the God of War, so you may not be too surprised to learn that their owner had fed them—ever since they were little bitty horses—on HUMAN FLESH. Disgusting! They were, to put it mildly, a menace. To all of Thrace. And beyond.

Herakles arrived on the scene and decided to gross them out entirely. He killed their owner AND his men and—did you guess?—FED THEM to the horses.

Freaked out, the horses immediately became tame. Herakles brought them back to Mycenae, though he always, ALWAYS kept a very close eye on them, especially when they got near his fingers, which were, he realized, perfect snacks.

HOW'S THAT AGAIN?

Ares **AIR-eez**

Diomedes **die-oh-MEE-deez**

Mycenae **my-SEE-nee**

Thrace **THRASE**

IX. THE GIRDLE OF THE AMAZONS

ASSIGNMENT: *Bring it back.*

OK: listen closely.

Hippolyta was the queen of the Amazons—fierce female warriors. She had been given a magic girdle by Ares, the God of War.

Before we go any further, let's get one thing straight: a magic girdle is probably not what you're thinking it is—it doesn't go with a magic bra. No, it's "an article of dress usually encircling the waist." This makes it more like a sash, or a big ribbon; call it a belt.

Now, the daughter of Eurystheus really, really wanted that magic girdle. So once again: labor time for Herakles.

Off he went to Kappadocia, where Hippolyta and her Amazons were hanging out. And lo and behold, Hippolyta simply GAVE him the magic girdle. Amazing!

Well, things are rarely that simple: troublemaking Hera started a whisper campaign that Herakles was going to kidnap Hippolyta and take her away.

This led to a terrible war between Herakles and the Amazons.

As usual, Herakles won—girdle in hand.

HOW'S THAT AGAIN?

Amazons
AM-a-zons

Ares
AIR-eez

Hippolyta
hip-POL-ih-tah

Kappadocia
kap-ah-DOE-chuh

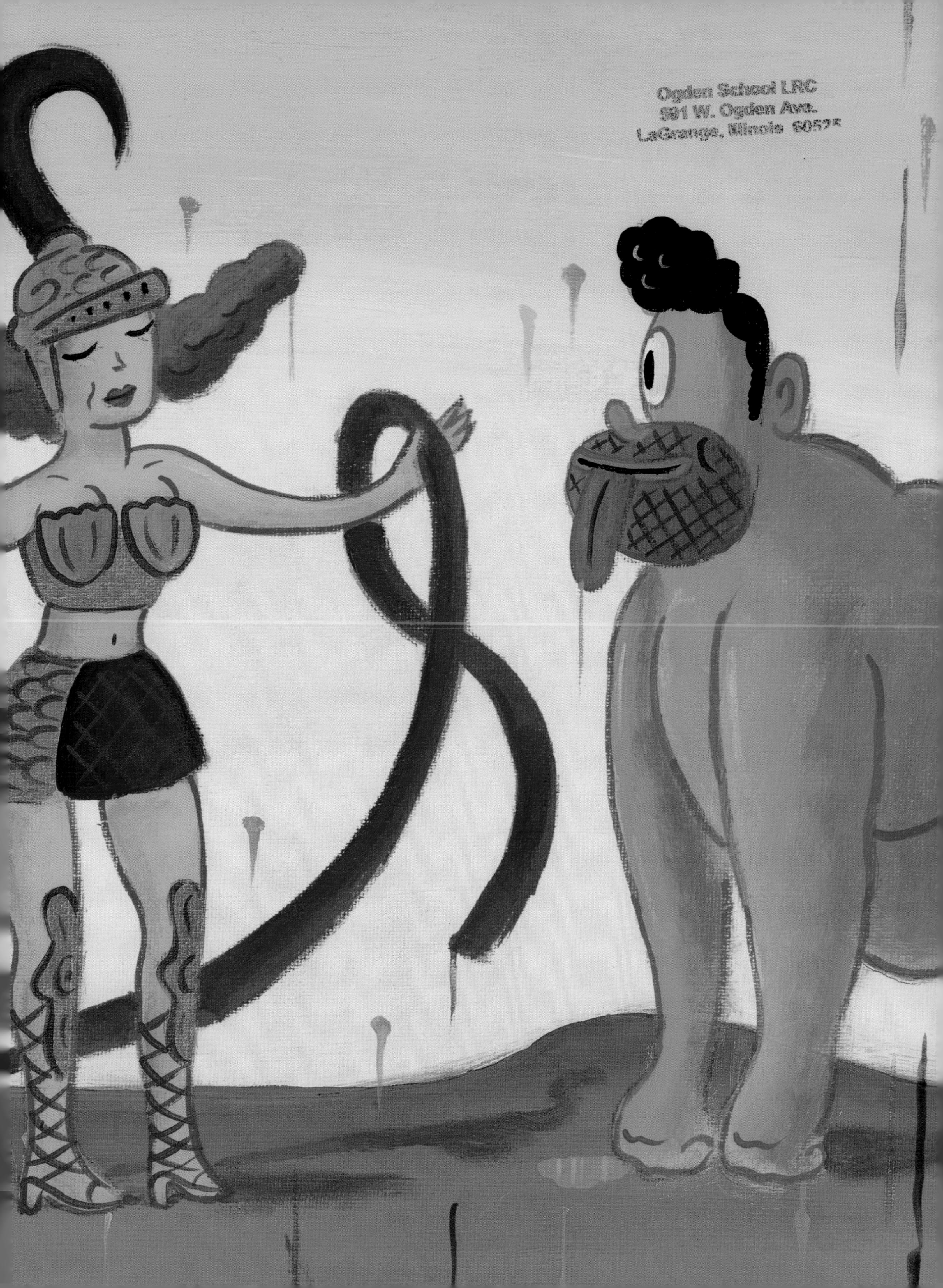

X. THE OXEN OF GERYON

ASSIGNMENT: *Bring them back.*

Oh man, this is complicated…

To begin with, Herakles, on assigment once again, traveled long and far to get to Iberia (today we call it Spain), where King Geryon kept his famous oxen. No one seems to know precisely what made them so famous. (Maybe they knew someone, or did tricks, or something.) Geryon himself was quite well known for having three bodies joined into one. Creepy!

First off, Herakles killed the man who watched over Geryon's oxen. Then—Herakles was on a roll now—he killed Geryon's two-headed dog, Orthros. Then he killed the three-bodied king. To celebrate, Herakles set up stone pillars at the very tip of Spain, and they're still called the Pillars of Herakles—a way of saying "Herakles Was Here."

For Herakles, killing things was a snap; now came the hard part: he had to bring the oxen of the dead King Geryon back to Mycenae.

The fun began immediately.

Hera—eternally cranky—sent a nasty fly that drove the oxen crazy. Needless to say, this made rounding them up a tremendous hassle for Herakles.

Finally, FINALLY, Herakles got the more-trouble-than-they're-worth oxen back to Greece. And what did Eurystheus do? Killed every single one as a sacrifice to Hera, who was no friend to our hero.

HOW'S THAT AGAIN?

Geryon
GAIR-ee-on

Mycenae
my-SEE-nee

Orthros
ORTH-ros

XI. CERBERUS

ASSIGNMENT: *Bring him back.*

By now Eurystheus was getting pretty tired of this give-a-labor-to-Herakles bit. Each time he hoped he had gotten rid of Herakles once and for all; and each time Herakles would return, triumphant. Eurystheus thought and thought and came up with an especially frightening labor for the legendary he-man.

He told Herakles he wanted the dog that guarded the gate to Hell itself: Cerberus. Big. Nasty. Three headed.

Off goes Herakles to Hades.

Hades is ruled by, well, Hades, the god of the Underworld. Hades wasn't thrilled about giving up his dog—who would be? So first Herakles had to defeat Hades (or wound him—even Herakles couldn't really kill a god). Then he turned his attention to Cerberus.

Cerberus was a handful, even for Herakles. But—just as he did with the Nemean Lion (Labor No. I)—Herakles tried the bare-knuckles approach, and it worked beautifully: he wrestled Cerberus to the ground, or the underground, and brought him back for Eurystheus to behold.

HOW'S THAT AGAIN?

Cerberus
SIR-bur-us

Hades
HAY-dees

XII. THE GOLDEN APPLES OF THE HESPERIDES

ASSIGNMENT: *Bring them back.*

Geography time! Where—or what?—are the Hesperides? They're actually nymphs (that is, beautiful maidens), but Herakles didn't have a clue where to find them. And no Hesperides… no Golden Apples. And the Golden Apples were what Herakles needed.

He decided to consult a spooky weirdo known as "The Old Man of the Sea," Nereus. It took strong persuasion to get Nereus to talk—he was a shape-shifter—but eventually Nereus came up with usable directions to the Garden of the Hesperides, which was located—of course—far, far away, at the edge of the world. And the Golden Apples—of course—were on a tree guarded by a snaky dragon named Ladon.

Off goes Herakles on adventure after adventure—pygmies, an eagle, the bad guy known as Antaeus…now *this* is interesting. Every time Antaeus's feet hit the ground, he would regain all his strength, because his mother was the Earth and he got his strength from her.

Herakles could be very smart when push came to shove, so to speak. He lifted Antaeus up OFF THE GROUND. With his feet no longer touching the earth, Antaeus—like you or me—pretty quickly got crushed to death in Herakles' iron grasp. Goodbye, Antaeus!

Herakles—with the help of Atlas, who carried the whole world on his shoulders—finally got his hands on the Golden Apples. In triumph, Herakles brought them back to Eurystheus. Eurystheus graciously gave them back to Herakles. Nonplussed, Herakles gave them to Athena, the Goddess of Wisdom, who didn't really need them, so Athena returned the Golden Apples to the Hesperides.

This may seem pretty pointless, but it's not: later on, in another adventure, Herakles would need those Golden Apples to get up to Mount Olympos.

HOW'S THAT AGAIN?

Antaeus **an-TAI-us**
Athena **ah-THEE-na**
Hesperides **hes-PAIR-id-ees**
Ladon **LAY-don**
Nereus **NAIR-ee-us**

ENOUGH WITH THE LABORS

At this point, Eurystheus decided to throw in the towel, though Herakles, unstoppable, just kept on going, until even he ran out of adventures.

He married the beautiful Hebe, the Goddess of Youth, and ended his days up on Mount Olympos, sipping nectar, a very cool beverage.

But that's another story.

THE END'

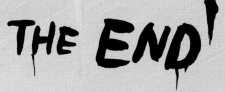

HOW'S THAT AGAIN?

Hebe **HE-be**

© 2005 J. Paul Getty Trust
Illustrations © 2005 Gary Baseman

Getty Publications
1200 Getty Center Drive
Suite 500
Los Angeles, California 90049-1682
www.getty.edu

Christopher Hudson, Publisher
Mark Greenberg, Editor in Chief

John Harris, Editor
Jim Drobka, Designer
Elizabeth Zozom, Production Coordinator

Library of Congress Cataloging-in-Publication Data

Harris, John, 1950 July 7-
  Strong stuff : Herakles and his labors / John Harris ;
illustrated by Gary Baseman.
      p. cm.
  ISBN 0-89236-784-9 (hardcover)
  ISBN 978-0-89236-784-9
  1. Heracles (Greek mythology)—Juvenile literature.
I. Baseman, Gary. II. Title.
  BL820.H5H37 2005
  398.2'0938'02—dc22
                              2004007904

Printed and bound by Tien Wah Press, Singapore

For Jim—JH

To my wife, Mel, who has the strength of an ant.
I mean, like an ant, she can carry four times her
body weight.—GB

THRACE

MOUNT OLYMPOS.

GREECE

AEGEAN SEA

DELPHI

•THEBES

MARATHON.

KERYNEIA

LAKE
STYMPHALOS•

•ATHENS

ELIS

MOUNT
ERYMANTHOS

NEMEA

MYCENAE

LERNA•

RIVER ALPHEUS

IONIAN SEA

← IBERIA
(ROUGHLY SPEAKING, MODERN-DAY SPAIN)

← PILLARS OF HERAKLES (NEAR IBERIA)

← GARDEN OF THE
HESPERIDES
(NOT ON ANY MAP)

↓ HADES (NOT ON ANY MAP)

CRETE

THE WORLD OF
HERAKLES